THE TIPTOEING TIGER

Philippa Leathers

CANDLEWICK PRESS

Everyone in the forest knew that tigers were sleek, silent, and totally terrifying. When a tiger prowled through the forest, everyone found other places to be.

But no one took any notice
of Little Tiger.

No one jumped when he roared.

No one ran away when he tumbled through the forest.

His brother laughed. "Oh, Little Tiger, you're too small and clumsy to scare anyone!"

"I am not!" said Little Tiger. "I'm sleek, silent, and totally terrifying."

His brother smiled. "I don't think you can scare a single animal in the forest."

"I can!" said Little Tiger. "And I'll prove it."

Little Tiger began to tiptoe through the forest
as silently as he could.

Tiptoe, tiptoe, tiptoe . . .

ROAR!!!

"You don't scare me," yawned Boar. "I could hear you coming a mile away."

"Bother!" said Little Tiger, and he set off again to find someone else to scare.

Tiptoe, tiptoe, tiptoe . . .

"Hello, Little Tiger," said Elephant.

"Did I scare you?" asked Little Tiger.

"Oh, no. You're much too small."

"Drat!" said Little Tiger, and he set off again
to find someone else to scare.

Tiptoe, tiptoe, tiptoe . . .

ROAR!

"Was that meant to scare us?" asked the monkeys, laughing.

"Yes, it was," said Little Tiger.

The monkeys just kept laughing.

Little Tiger felt sad. *I may not be sleek, silent, or totally terrifying,* he thought. *But I WILL find someone to scare!*

Just then a frog jumped—*SPLOSH!*—into a pond. *This is my chance,* thought Little Tiger. *I can scare that tiny, jumpy frog.*

He crept silently up to the water's edge.

Tiptoe, tiptoe, tiptoe . . .

"Oh, help!" cried Little Tiger.

Bravely, Little Tiger tiptoed back to the
water's edge and slowly peered into the pond.

A tiger — sleek, silent, and totally terrifying — peered back.

"Well, Little Tiger?" asked his brother. "Did you scare anyone?"

"As a matter of fact, I did," said Little Tiger.

"Myself!"

FOR ROWAN!!!

First edition 2018

Library of Congress Catalog Card Number pending
ISBN 978-0-7636-8843-1

18 19 20 21 22 TLF 10 9 8 7 6 5 4 3 2

Printed in Dongguan, Guangdong, China

This book was typeset in ITC Mendoza Roman.
The illustrations were done in pencil and watercolor, combined digitally.

Candlewick Press
99 Dover Street
Somerville, Massachusetts 02144

visit us at www.candlewick.com